JEWEL STICKER STORIES

THE Littlest Mermaid

By Wendy Cheyette Lewison

Illustrated by Jerry Smath

To Carrie Miller from her grandpa—J.S.

Grosset & Dunlap • New York

Text copyright © 1997 by Grosset & Dunlap, Inc. Illustrations copyright © 1997 by Jerry Smath. All rights reserved. Published by Grosset & Dunlap, Inc., a member of Penguin Putnam Books for Young Readers, New York. GROSSET & DUNLAP is a trademark of Grosset & Dunlap, Inc. Published simultaneously in Canada. Printed in the U.S.A.

ISBN 0-448-41596-8   C D E F G H I J

Once there was a wonderful undersea world where the mermaids lived. One mermaid was the littlest of all. She had bright blue eyes the color of the sea, and pretty golden hair, like sparkling sunshine in the water.

Can you find the littlest mermaid? When you do, put a sticker on her headband to make it shine!

The other mermaids were always busy doing
what mermaids do. They did not have time for
the littlest mermaid. So when nighttime came,
she would sit on her rock under the stars, and
wish very hard for a friend.

Put a sticker on a star to make it twinkle.

Every day she looked for a friend. She looked
as she played in the coral reef garden.

Which flower do you think is the prettiest? Put a pretty sticker on it.

She looked for a friend while she rode around and around on the mermaid merry-go-round.

Pick out your favorite sea horse.
Put a colorful sticker on it.

In an old sunken ship, she saw a chest full of treasure—sparkling diamonds, shimmering emeralds, glittering gold.

Fill the treasure chest with shiny sticker treasure!

In a dark, dark cave, she found a wiggly octopus.
He offered her a cup of tea. But she did not want
octopus tea.

Light up her lantern with a sticker so she can see in the dark, dark cave.

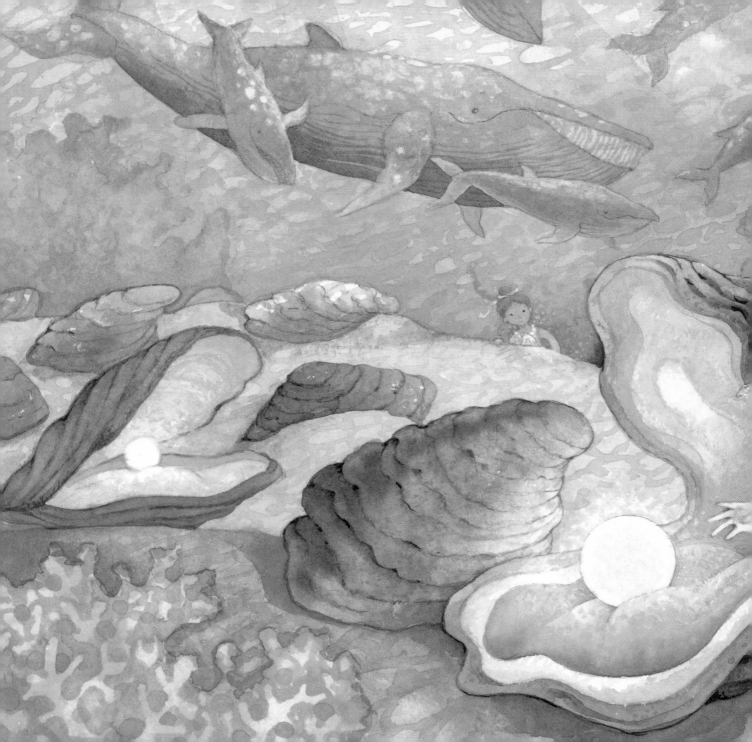

She found a lustrous pearl in the oyster bed.

**Put a sticker
on the pearl
to make it glow.**

She found the prettiest fish she had ever seen.
It was bright orange and had black stripes all over.
But she did not see a friend anywhere.

Put a pretty, shiny sticker on the
mermaid's favorite fish.

The littlest mermaid went to sleep at night still wishing and wishing for a friend. One morning, there was a surprise waiting for her. It was a beautiful shell necklace! Where had it come from? Do you know?

Put a special sticker on the surprise necklace, and it will glitter.

It was a gift from another little mermaid who had been watching her all the time—and wishing for a friend, too! Can you find her now?

Put a sticker on the
littlest mermaid's new friend.

The two little mermaids played together, happy
at last in the shiny, briny mermaid world.

Make everything sparkle
and shine with lots of stickers!

And the littlest mermaid wore her gift
of friendship forever after.